PHILIPPA PEARCE

Emily's Own Elephant

Illustrated by John Lawrence

Greenwillow Books

NEW YORK

TO MY DAUGHTER, SALLY, WHOSE STORY

THIS WAS LONG AGO

Text copyright © 1987 by Philippa Pearce
Illustrations copyright © 1987 by John Lawrence
First published in Great Britain in 1987 by Julia MacRae Books
Published in the United States in 1988
All rights reserved. No part of this book may be reproduced
or utilized in any form or by any means, electronic or mechanical,
including photocopying, recording or by any information storage
and retrieval system, without permission in writing from the
Publisher, Greenwillow Books, a division of William Morrow & Company, Inc.,
105 Madison Avenue, New York, N.Y. 10016.
Printed in Italy   First American Edition   1 2 3 4 5 6 7 8 9 10

Library of Congress Cataloging-in-Publication Data
Pearce, Philippa.   Emily's own elephant.
Summary: When the zoo is unable to keep a miniature elephant,
Emily and her parents make a home for it and its monkey friend
in their lovely meadow with a river running by.
[1. Elephants—Fiction] I. Lawrence, John, 1933– ill.
II. Title.   PZ7.P3145Em 1987   [E]   87-14039
ISBN 0-688-07678-5   ISBN 0-688-07679-3 (lib. bdg.)

CHAPTER I   *The Meadow with the Shed*

Emily lived with her mother and father in a little house
in the corner of a big meadow. A river ran along one side of
the meadow.

Huge trees grew in the meadow. There were oaks and chestnuts and sycamores and ash-trees. Emily's father used to say: "There are far too many trees in the meadow. Perhaps I should cut some of them down."

His wife said: "You haven't enough to do in your spare time.
That's why you want to go cutting trees down."

A big shed stood in the meadow. It was old, but it was not in ruins. There were no holes in the roof for the rain to come through. There were no holes in the walls for the wind to blow through. The shed was quite empty. It was not used for anything.

Emily's father said: "Perhaps I should pull that useless shed down."

Emily's mother said: "You haven't enough to do in your spare time. That's why you want to go pulling sheds down."

Emily said: "Don't cut the trees down. Don't pull the shed down. You never know when we may need trees and an empty shed."

Emily's father promised not to cut down the trees or pull down the shed just yet.

CHAPTER 2   *Emily visits the Zoo*

One day in winter Emily went to London to visit the Zoo.
She went with her mother. They saw all the animals that Emily
liked best: the lions, the tigers, the hippos, the rhinos, the camels,
the giraffes, the elephants, the wolves and the panda-bear.

Then it was time for tea, and they went to the cafeteria. Emily's mother had a pot of tea and a packet of biscuits, and Emily had an icecream and a packet of potato crisps.

When they had finished tea, Emily's mother said : "It's nearly time to go home. Is there anything else you very much want to see, Emily?"

"Yes," said Emily. "I want to go to the Children's Zoo."

They visited the goats, and Emily fed one
with a sandwich. The goat ate the sandwich,
and then it ate the paper-bag, and then
it tried to eat the glove on the hand that
had held the sandwich and the paper-bag.

So they went to the Children's Zoo.
They saw the rabbits and Emily stroked one.
They watched the chickens hatching out
of eggs.

Then Emily and her mother came to a special enclosure with
a baby elephant in it. It was the nicest elephant that
Emily had ever seen.

A keeper was standing by the elephant's enclosure. Emily asked him: "What is the baby elephant called?"

"Jumbo," said the keeper.

"Jumbo!" said Emily's mother. "What a nice name! Now, Emily, it's time to go home."

The keeper said to Emily: "We are very worried about Jumbo."
"Why?" said Emily.

"Come along, Emily," said her mother.

The keeper said to Emily: "We are worried about Jumbo because he doesn't grow. He is strong and he is healthy, but he simply won't grow. He is going to be a miniature elephant."

"I didn't know that elephants could be miniature," said Emily.

"*Come along, Emily*," said her mother.

"It happens only very, very rarely," said the keeper. "But it is always very awkward. The Zoo wants only elephants that are elephantine in size. It can't keep a miniature elephant."

"Oh," said Emily.

"COME ALONG, EMILY," said her mother.

"We shall have to find a home for Jumbo," said the keeper.

"EMILY!" said Emily's mother very loudly and crossly.

Emily usually did what her mother told her, especially as her mother usually told her to do only sensible things. So now Emily began to follow her mother out of the Children's Zoo.

Then Emily stopped. "I'm sorry," she said to her mother, "but we can't go home yet. I have an important idea. I must discuss it with the keeper. I must go back now."

So back they went.

CHAPTER 3 *The Plan*

They went back to the baby elephant's enclosure. The keeper was still
standing there. He was looking at Jumbo in a worried way.

Emily said: "You told us that you would have to find a home for Jumbo."

"Yes," said the keeper.

"We could give him a home," said Emily, and she looked at her mother.

Emily's mother said to the keeper: "My daughter is quite right.
We should be delighted to give your little elephant a home."

The keeper said: "That's very kind of you; but even a miniature
elephant needs a great deal of space."

"Would a big meadow do?" asked Emily's mother.

"A really big meadow," said Emily.

"Yes," said the keeper, "a really big meadow would do. But even a miniature elephant needs a lot of water to drink and to bathe in and to squirt around when it plays."

"Would a river running by the meadow do?" Emily asked.

'Yes," said the keeper, "a river would do. But what about when it rains – what about when it rains bucketfuls and blows gales? The little elephant will need shelter then."

"Would a shed in the meadow do?" asked Emily.

"A really big shed," said her mother. "It has no holes in the roof or the walls, and it's quite empty."

"Yes," said the keeper, "a really big shed would do."

"Then that's settled," said Emily's mother.

"Wait!" said the keeper. "What about when it snows and freezes: would your shed be warm enough for a little elephant then?"

"No," said Emily. "Our shed hasn't a coal-fire; it hasn't a gas-fire; it hasn't an electric fire."

"Wait," said Emily's mother. "We could put in central heating."

"Wouldn't that be very expensive?" said Emily.

"It would be worth it," said her mother. "It's not often anyone has the chance of a baby elephant that will stay small."

"That's settled then," said the keeper. "We are very grateful to you. There's just one more thing."

"What is that?"

"Jumbo will be lonely without any of his friends," said the keeper. "Could you take one of his friends as well?"

"What kind of friend?" asked Emily's mother.

"His best friend is a baby monkey called Jacko. He likes climbing," said the keeper.

"Then he can climb all the trees in the meadow," said Emily's mother.

"I've always longed for a little elephant and a monkey," said Emily.

"When they are old enough," said the keeper, "Jumbo and Jacko will come to you in a special Zoo van. Please write your name and address on this paper."

So they did, and then they went home.

CHAPTER 4   *Friends in the Meadow*

One Saturday in summer Emily's father was eating toast and
marmalade and looking out of the window.

Suddenly he spoke with his mouth full: "There is a big van, like a horse-box,
at the gate into our meadow. Two men are driving the van into our meadow.
Now they are opening the van. Something is coming out. OH! OH! OH!"

Emily's father nearly choked on his toast and marmalade. He said:

"There is an elephant in our meadow, with a monkey on its back!"

Then Emily and her mother told him all about Jumbo and Jacko. They had been keeping the secret to surprise him.

He was delighted. He said: "We must be sure to have the central heating in the shed before next winter. I will put it in myself. That will save expense."

"It will also give you something to do in your spare time," said his wife.

Then they all went into the meadow with buns for the elephant and bananas for the monkey. They took a pot of tea for the Zoo men, and a big plum cake that happened to be in the house. There was a slice for everybody, and sugar biscuits too, and chocolate fingers. They all had a picnic together in the sunshiny meadow.

Then the Zoo men said goodbye and went home. Emily's mother went indoors to make more buns. Emily's father went up the village to the Public Library to borrow a book about central heating.

Emily was left alone in the meadow with Jumbo and Jacko. It
was very hot, so Emily led the way to the river. Jumbo waded in the
cool water and squirted it over his friends. They loved this.

Then Jacko went racing through the tree-tops.
He picked armfuls of pink and white blossom from
the very tops of the chestnut-trees. It was the
biggest and best chestnut blossom that Emily had
ever seen. She made wreaths and garlands and chains
of it for Jumbo and Jacko and herself.

Then they began to dance round and round the meadow.
Emily's mother finished baking her buns and came into the meadow to
watch. Emily's father came home with his book on central heating
and went into the meadow, too. Emily's father and mother stood and
watched and laughed and clapped. And round and round the meadow danced
Emily and her two friends from the Zoo.